Clifford
Takes a Walk

W9-CDY-853

Happy Halloween
Stay safe !

Love,

Reaga

Norman Bridwell

For the teachers who have been helping children learn to read with Clifford for over fifty years.

The Bridwells would like to thank Frank Rocco for his contributions to this book.

For information regarding permission, write to Scholastic Inc., Attention: Permissions Department, 557 Broadway, New York, NY 10012.

This book is a work of fiction. Names, characters, places, and incidents are either the product of the author's imagination or are used fictitiously, and any resemblance to actual persons, living or dead, business establishments, events, or locales is entirely coincidental.

ISBN 978-0-545-92398-9

10 9 8 7 6 5 4 3 2   16 17 18 19

Printed in the U.S.A.   40

First printing 2015

SCHOLASTIC INC.

Hi! I'm Emily Elizabeth. This is my dog, Clifford, and these are some of my classmates. We're waiting for it to be safe to cross the street so we can start our school day.

Our teacher, Ms. Tate, has a treat for us today!

"This is Ms. Patel from Safe Kids," Ms. Tate tells us. "She knows everything about road safety. We are going on a field trip with a surprise ending. On our way, Ms. Patel is going to help us practice the rules of being a safe walker."

Everyone is excited—especially Clifford!

Ms. Patel goes over the safe walking tips with us before we leave.

Ms. Tate tells us to find a walking partner. I choose Clifford.

Then she tells us we have to make a few stops on the way to help with our surprise. I can't wait to find out what it is!

"What's the number one rule of being a safe walker?"
Ms. Patel asks us before we leave.

We all know this one!

*"When crossing the street it's always a must
to walk along with an adult you trust."*

We are walking on the sidewalk when Clifford sees his friend Buster across the street. He is so happy that he runs into the road to say hi. "Clifford!" I call out. "It's not safe to run out into the road!"

"That's right," Ms. Patel says as Clifford comes back.
"Does anyone remember the next rule?"

I do!

*"Look left, right, left, and meet the driver's eye
to make sure you're noticed before you cross by."*

Ms. Patel says I did a great job!

Our first stop is the grocery store. The clerk hands Ms. Tate a bag.

I wonder what is in the bag!

"Is everyone ready to go?" Ms. Patel asks the class.

"Yes!" we say.

Clifford is so excited he keeps wagging his tail back and forth. But when we come to a street corner, we all stop. Even Clifford!

"Who remembers what rule we are following?" Ms. Patel asks.

My friend Sam raises his hand.

"It's best not to cross in the middle of the block. Go to the corner and use the crosswalk."

"This is our next stop!" Ms. Tate announces as we come to the sports store down the block.

"I wonder what she needs to get here," I whisper to Clifford. He sniffs the ground for clues.

The store clerk hands Ms. Tate two shopping bags.
She gives one bag to Nate and one bag to Rosa to carry.

"Don't look inside the bags," Ms. Tate says. "You don't want to ruin your surprise!"

Just then, Nate accidentally drops his bag. A yellow rubber ball rolls out and into the street.

Clifford wants to play with the ball, so he runs after it!

"Clifford, no!" I cry. "Remember the rule?
It's up to you to make the right call.
Don't dart in the street to chase that ball!"
"Great job, Emily Elizabeth," Ms. Patel says.

Our last stop is across the street at the pet store.

"Who knows what to do at a corner without a traffic light?" Ms. Patel asks.

Before anyone can answer, Clifford smells something and puts out a paw to cross the street!

"Clifford, stay here!" we yell.

"Wherever you walk it's important that you look for cars that are turning and backing up, too!"

"That's right!" Ms. Patel says after Clifford is back on the sidewalk.

At the pet store, the clerk hands Ms. Tate one last bag.
"Are we going to find out what the surprise is now?" I ask.
"Very soon!" she says.

After a few minutes, we reach another corner. There is a lot of traffic but no traffic light. We wait and wait for the cars to stop.

"Ms. Patel, when will those cars stop so we can cross the street for our surprise?" Gabriel asks.

Suddenly, Clifford notices something in the grass and starts sniffing. "Of course!" says Ms. Tate. "There is supposed to be a STOP sign here. It must have fallen over."

"Stop signs are big and red," says Ms. Patel. "They act like a red light: Drivers know they have to stop when they see one."

But without the stop sign, how will the cars know to stop?

Just then, Clifford picks up the stop sign with his mouth and walks over to the corner.

"Great idea, Clifford!" Ms. Patel says.

Now that big, red Clifford is holding the big, red stop sign, the drivers know exactly what to do.

The driver of the delivery truck stops, and everyone can safely cross the street!

Clifford saved the day!

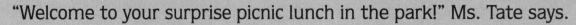

"Welcome to your surprise picnic lunch in the park!" Ms. Tate says.

"You are now all super safe walkers—especially Clifford!" Ms. Patel says.

We eat lunch and play with the toys from the sports store. There's even a yummy treat for Clifford.

This is the best surprise field trip ever!